GHOUTA

Snehaal Kemal

NewDelhi • London

BLUEROSE PUBLISHERS
India | U.K.

Copyright © Snehaal Kemal 2025

All rights reserved by author. No part of this publication may be reproduced, stored in a retrieval system or transmitted in any form or by any means, electronic, mechanical, photocopying, recording or otherwise, without the prior permission of the author. Although every precaution has been taken to verify the accuracy of the information contained herein, the publisher assumes no responsibility for any errors or omissions. No liability is assumed for damages that may result from the use of information contained within.

BlueRose Publishers takes no responsibility for any damages, losses, or liabilities that may arise from the use or misuse of the information, products, or services provided in this publication.

For permissions requests or inquiries regarding this publication, please contact:

BLUEROSE PUBLISHERS
www.BlueRoseONE.com
info@bluerosepublishers.com
+91 8882 898 898
+4407342408967

ISBN: 978-93-7018-020-8

First Edition: April 2025

This is a love story of Fatima, a Syrian woman. Her journey through life and the hardship she faced during the Syrian civil conflict. Her life drastically changed due to the war. She lost everything and still flows with her life like a river flowing. She finds her soul mate, John in her life's journey, who brings meaning to her existence. John, a mystical man who is enveloped by experiences of life, investigates the significance of a tranquil human existence in the context of humanity's conflicts...

Dedicated to all the innocent beings, who lost their lives, suffered pain and difficulties, when they were caught in between the wars of egos and ideologies.

TABLE OF CONTENTS-

1. CHAPTER ONE- IBRAHIM

2. CHAPTER TWO- FATIMA

3. CHAPTER THREE- GHOUTA

4. CHAPTER FOUR- THE REFUGEE

5. CHAPTER FIVE- ISTANBUL

6. CHAPTER SIX- NOOR- E-SHAMS

7. CHAPTER 7- JOHN

8. CHAPTER 8- ADMIRAL RUSTOM PASHA

9. CHAPTER 9- RUMI

10. CHAPTER 10- DR. HASHIM

11. CHAPTER 11- ZULU

Al- Raqqah

Before War

After War

Chapter 1

Ibrahim

It was January 2011, and the wheat harvest was getting ready for the next spring. Ibrahim smiled broadly as he stared at the tall, green wheat crops.

"The harvest is likely to be fantastic this year. We'll have a fantastic spring this year." he murmured, clutching the damp clay of his field in his fist.

His son Nasser nodded in accord. "Allah hu Akbar."

"Amen." Ibrahim affirmed.

Ibrahim was a short stature man with a broad face and broad shoulders. He was respected and well known in his village. He was a peon at the local school, who retired prematurely to follow his passion for farming after his daughter's marriage.

Ibrahim was born into a farming family in the village of Al-Sahl, a small settlement tucked in the hills west of Al-Raqqah. Al-Raqqah was located in northern Syria, on the banks of the Euphrates River.

Wheat harvests have been low in recent years due to an ongoing drought and decreasing water streams in the Euphrates River.

"This canal from the river saved our crops this time. Long live Bashar, who saved our crops by building this small canal from the Tabqa Dam," Ibrahim exclaimed, gazing up at the hot sun.

Nasser, the obedient son, nodded again.

"This year, I'll get you married. Your sister is doing well in Goutha after her marriage last year. I hope to find a suitable girl for you. I believe Zainab, the cobbler's daughter, is a suitable match. Abu Rasheed has opened a new shoe shop here, in the Raqqah bazaar. His status now matches ours. I'll go to his house and ask for his daughter's hand for you. Your sister called me yesterday and told me that they are planning to have a baby next year. I am glad she has a well-educated husband, as she herself has a degree in languages." Ibrahim told his son as they walked back home through the narrow lanes of Raqqah bazaar.

"Your mother is diabetic." Her legs are bloated, and the left leg has an ulcer. Yesterday, the doctor at the general hospital informed me that it was a diabetic foot. "She may need to have her left leg amputated before the infection spreads," Ibrahim added, taking a deep breath and sighing.

Ibrahim had no idea how much this spring would affect his life. But Nasser's mind was filled with memories of what he was taught at Madarsaa in Mosul. He had visited Mosul last month along with his friend. He was highly influenced by the teacher, named Abu Baghdadi, at the school in Mosul.

The father and son strolled along the small lanes of Al Sahl to their home, which was at the end of Central Street in the village.

The news of the Arab Spring spreading throughout the Arab world was being broadcast on television. They followed the happenings in Tunisia with surprise and horror. The fire eventually reached neighboring countries.

"Our Syria is a peaceful country." Look at Iraq, which has been blazing for years. There is fighting in both Palestine and Lebanon. No one talks about our land of Shams," Ibrahim said with a sense of pride for his homeland. Sipping a cup of 'chay' [tea], he declared loudly, "Syria is a land of peace, and Allah bestows all mercy on our land." Our country is thriving and is doing well.

He couldn't understand that some sandstorms are strong enough to cover the entire desert, not just a portion of it.

It began with tiny, nonviolent protests in 'Darra', south of Damascus. The protest was against the regime's policies on jobs and corruption. Then a protest took place in Damascus. The protests began in modest numbers at first, but soon spread to other cities across Syria. Young individuals with warm blood and vigor flocked to the streets to join the demonstration. They wanted things to change. There was excitement in the air as more young Syrians joined, until the authorities cracked down on demonstrators.

The protests quickly turned violent, and intermittent protests turned into daily violent incidents. The death toll began to mount, and a cycle of rage, vengeance, and wrath began to play out. One event triggered another, and the chain of events pushed the country into a full-fledged civil war.

Al Sahl was not immune to similar incidents either. Ibrahim backed the administration, but his son Nasser viewed things differently. He desired change.

"Father, if they had built the trench from the dam to our fields many years ago, we would be wealthier and drive expensive cars like the great families of Damascus." We, too, could have lead a wonderful life. "But now we are struggling to make ends meet," he continued, disputing with Ibrahim.

The fire on the streets had now spread inside their home.

Ibrahim continued with his farming. While he was concerned about the price of wheat he would fetch in local bazaar, his son, Nasser, joined the Free Syrian Army (FSA) to participate in the revolutionary movement. Nasser aspired to be a police officer but gave up when he began to struggle in school, after he returned from Mosul. Ibrahim accused him of associating with hardliners when the principal summoned him to a parent-teacher meeting at the school.

The formerly docile son has turned rebellious.

Chapter 2

Fatima

The winds of change have begun to blow. Following the Arab Spring in Tunisia, the storm arrived in Syria in 2011.

"It will envelop my whole country." Ahmed spoke to Fatima while watching TV, holding a lamb bone in his hand.

"Ya Allah," Fatima remarked, glancing at the news on their television.

"Come on, Ahmed; nothing will happen here in Damascus. Eat peacefully now." Fatima swiftly added.

Fatima was 26 when she married Ahmed, who was 33. In her village, daughters were normally married off before the age of 18, so marriage at older age was unusual.

Ahmed has been taking care of his mother and younger brother since his father's death when he was in eighth grade. He couldn't even consider marriage until he purchased a home in "Darra" for his mother and younger brother. He later relocated to Goutha, a suburban area near Damascus, in quest of better chances of livelihood after completing his graduation in chemical engineering. Ahmed was now a chemical engineer working for a Syrian oil business.

Fighting had begun a few months ago between Assad's forces and the Free Syrian Army. But in Goutha, life was normal. Fatima and her husband, Ahmed, supported the Free Syrian Army. In a divided country, it was simple to select sides.

"Won't we support the Free Syrian Army? After all, we are Sunnis like them, believers in the Prophet's [peace be upon him] rightful successors," Fatima told Ahmed as she sipped chay at the dining table.

Fatima and Ahmed now live in an apartment complex across the main road in Ghouta. Their apartment was on the fifth floor of "Noor-e-Manzil," from which Fatima could see Damascus' beautiful skyline and sunrise.

Ahmed was extremely supportive of Fatima's career. He helped her in start a language school in Ghouta's Al-Nasser Street residential complex. She also completed her postgraduate studies following their wedding last year. Fatima immediately recruited enough students, largely children from nearby neighborhoods, and began teaching them English and Arabic.

Every evening, after school, she would sit on her flat's balcony, drinking her favorite drink, an orange juice, and watching people pass by on Main Street.

In that leisure time she would get lost in thoughts of her of her life at Raqqah. Ibrahim, her father was fond of oranges too. The elderly man often brought her oranges from his friend's farm in the village of Abbara, near Raqqa. Fatima was proud of her father for supporting her through college and postgraduate education. Only a few individuals in her ancestral village favored higher education for women.

The elders of Al Sahl used to tell Fatima whenever she went to social gatherings that "Islam forbids women's education; they should always be covered in hijab and look after their husbands and children." the elders of Al Sahl used to tell Fatima whenever she went to social gatherings. However, it was her father who always stood by her in such struggles.

The first six months of Fatima's marriage were like living in a timeless "Jannat." Before the fire reached her city's outskirts, she fantasized about the kid she would have, wanting to name him 'Ahmed the junior' after her husband's name.

One Monday, Ahmed arrived home early for lunch. Fatima was surprised because he typically comes home around 5 p.m. She arranged the chicken stew, soup, and kebabs on the dinner table. Ahmed always used to ask her to sit beside him, while eating the food on the table.

"I have a surprise for you." He said

After the lunch, he called her close and said "Come with me, Fatima. I want to teach you a new thing."

He grabbed her hand and guided her to the parking lot of the apartment building. "Look, this is our new Ford car," Ahmed explained, opening the door and pushing her inside. Fatima was pleased and almost in tears.

She had wanted to learn to drive since she was a child, but Ibrahim refused to teach her.

"Oh, no, I will not teach you here in Al Sahl. The elders have already begun calling me names and chastising me for sending you to college. Let your husband teach you how to drive," he replied whenever she insisted.

The couple took a long trip on the main road and arrived at an abandoned Maidan near Damascus. The Maidan, which was usually bustling with children playing, has suddenly been vacant since the past few weeks.

"Do you understand, Fatima, the situation is tense here. Parents no longer send their children to playgrounds. Anyway, it's excellent for you. "A novice driver can learn more easily here without the risk of colliding with someone," Ahmed stated, turning the car into the Maidan via the huge gate.

Ahmed climbed out of the driver's seat and pulled her behind the wheel. He swiftly moved to the adjacent seat and began providing directions.

"This is the clutch, that's the accelerator, and that's the brake." You simply have to change gears based on the car's speed." He said.

"I'll teach you here every day until I find a suitable female driving instructor for you." It's more practical to wear a Capri or jeans under your hijab while driving," Ahmed added, gripping the steering wheel.

Ahmed continued to come home early in the evenings, driving Fatima to the Maidan every day to teach her how to drive, until he found a female driving instructor. This new shared experience added vibrancy to their marital lives. They had wonderful love moments, while the world outside was filled with hatred and anger.

Fatima was originally hesitant and terrified to drive, but it became easier with the careful supervision of a female driving instructor.

The azans from the mosques became louder, and religious gatherings swelled in number. People whispered more behind closed doors, and women began to wear hijabs more regularly, encouraging others to do the same.

The war began with gunfire and explosions shattering through the night's calm. Fatima looked out her balcony and saw the once-tall structures that dominated Damascus' skyline reduced to rubble. The night sky was illuminated by explosions and fires in the distance. The noises of helicopters or fighter jets pierced her ears with horror and vibrated her entire body. Sleep no longer came easily. Ahmed, too, sleeping beside her, often turned restless in his sleep.

"Fatima, one day we'll have to leave this building and move to a bunker nearby. Mohamed informed me that they've built bunkers for protection. The sooner we move, the better," Ahmed said in a hushed voice.

"I want to buy some new clothes from Mohamed. I saw him drying a new design dress on the terrace of his house yesterday," Fatima said, looking out the balcony.

Mohamed was a tall, skinny man in his sixties, always wearing a Syrian cap and combing his long white beard with a small comb from his shirt pocket. He was from a family of artisans known for their Syrian-designed clothing. He lived at the end of the street in his large ancestral house with a large front garden.

Soon, the war flames surrounded Fatima's home. By 2013, all of Syria was in flames. The Free Syrian Army, ISIS, and other factions fought each other and Bashar's government troops. Ghouta had strong support for the Free Syrian Army (FSA). The majority of the population was Sunni, providing strong support for the FSA. Ghouta became a key area of resistance to Damascus, the Syrian capital and seat of Bashar's government. Bashar, an 'Alawite,' was considered kafir by many hardliners and the Brotherhood followers.

No doubt, Ghouta was soon surrounded by government forces. From her balcony, Fatima saw nearby buildings crumbling under bombardment.

"We will shortly relocate to the bunkers. They have prepared some bunkers at the nearby school. We will shift there on Friday," Ahmed said.

Damascus

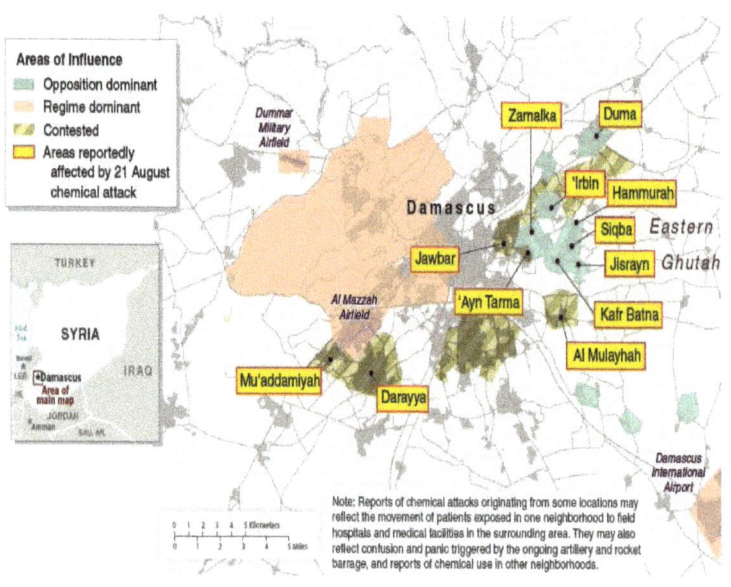

Ghouta

Chapter 3

Ghouta

Eastern Ghouta was located on the outskirts of Damascus. Fatima resided in the Zamalka district of Eastern Ghouta. The overwhelming majority of the people were Sunnis. It served as a strong base for rebels and was among the main supply routes for weaponry from Jordan. The rebels depended largely on this route in their struggle against the government. Undoubtedly, the government heavily shelled the route to counter the resistance.

The night of August 20, 2013, was unusually darker than other nights for the season. Ahmed returned home early that day. Due to the disturbances, he now arrives home earlier than usual.

Fatima made stewed soup and kebab for dinner, including "gohst" [mutton]. Sporadic power supplies triggered by wrecked power lines had turned off the lights. Power outages had become a common phenomenon. So, Fatima lit the candle at the dining table.

"It appears as an especially dark night that follows," Fatima said quietly.
Ahmed was gazing at the skyline from the balcony.
"Come inside, Ahmed. Let ourselves enjoy a candlelight meal tonight," Fatima said, placing cutlery on the dining table.
Ahmed pulled out a chair and answered, "Fatima, it's a very romantic night with a candlelight dinner, sparklers in the background, and a beautiful damsel seated beside me. It appears that this entire universe is celebrating our love."

Fatima blushed and wished to know "Aren't we heading to the bunkers tomorrow morning? I have packed the essentials. It's frightening to live above ground when everything else is being transformed into a plain Maidan."

"Indeed, we are," Ahmed replied.

"Insha Allah, everything will be fine," she said.
After dinner, they went directly to the bedroom and fell asleep in each other's arms.
Around 2:30 a.m. on the 23rd of August, Fatima heard screaming coming from down the stairs.
"Some folks are yelling and crying downstairs. Wake up, Ahmed! she said, patting his shoulder.
Ahmed hastily sprang up to Almira to wear his pants.

"You stay here. Don't come outside until I come back. I'll go downstairs to see what's happened," he said.

He opened the front door and rushed downstairs. Fatima could still hear children's screams and cries. Someone yelled, "Its gas!" It is a gas attack! "Go upstairs; don't come down."

Because the gas is heavier than the air, it will settle closer to the earth. She thought.

Fatima closed herself in the bathroom, turned on the shower, and drenched herself until the water in the overhead tank ran out.

She heard more screaming across the street, as well as ambulance sirens downstairs.

"Where's Ahmed? Everything is silent now. He has not come back," she thought.

She stayed there till 5:00 a.m. She heard someone's footstep coming upstairs and knocking on the door.

"Please open the door," someone urged.

She hurried to open the door. A medic and a firefighter entered the apartment and inquired if there were any children.

"Take this gas mask and come with us," the medic instructed.

"My husband went downstairs and did not return," Fatima told them.

"We'll find him down the stairs or across the street," the firefighter said.

Fatima spotted children's and women's bodies on the ground floor. Their eyeballs had popped out. She noticed a white froth stained with blood dripping from a child's mouth. A woman's tongue peeked out, and her eyes rolled up. Spasms had stretched another woman's body

Fatima wanted to scream, but she couldn't. Her speech was muffled by the gas mask.

As she reached the street, a medic directed her to get inside the ambulance.

He informed her, "We will transport you to a nearby hospital where the injured are receiving treatment."

"But my husband is here". Fatima said

"You will be able to identify your husband there," he stated.

They carried her to the hospital and washed her with a bucket of water in a room next to the emergency department.

A nurse approached and examined her thoroughly. "You seem to be fine," she said, taking a drug injection from a vial.

"You don't need this, but we will monitor your symptoms." The nurse then departed from the room.
Fatima, lying on the wet stretcher, had no idea when she fell asleep.
She woke later in the afternoon and noticed that the room was filled with other patients. She was exhausted but desperate to find her husband.

She asked the nurse, "Where can I find my husband?"
The nurse said, "You can go to the male ward, where the survivors are being treated." It's just at the end of the corridor.
She leaped off the stretcher and rushed to the ward, but could not see her man. She could only see dozens of children and older men struggling for a breathe in the clogged hospital, saline vials dangling above their heads and oxygen cylinders adjacent to their stretchers.
She asked the medic, "My husband isn't her; where else could I find him?"

"Go to the basement, in one big hall, they are being kept and counted." he responded.

She headed downstairs and discovered a man keeping track of the bodies. They were laid in a vast hall.
"You can look at the faces," he said, pointing at the face peeking out of the white cloth.
She dashed along the passage amid rows of corpses. He lay quietly in the corner of a row. She dropped to his feet, which were visible through the white cloth that covered his body. Sobbing quietly, she sat there for an hour.

The man, in charge of the mortuary approached to lift the devastated Fatima.
"Do not touch his feet, sister. Sarin gas is poisonous. Toxic," he cautioned.
He led her to the ground floor and told her to sit on the airport chairs placed in the corridor.
He exclaimed, "Ya Allah, the merciful," before leaving.

Fatima sat throughout the night in the corridor, her gaze locked on the wall in front of her. Memories flooded her mind, along with thoughts of an uncertain future. Tears filled her swollen eyes. She fell asleep in the chair and woke to the sound of the morning azan.
The deceased were laid to rest at the local cemetery. Corpses lay heaped on top of one another.
Fatima went home, only to see the wreckage of abandoned apartments.

"They are carrying the refugees to the Turkish border in buses this evening." I

think we ought to flee this place. "There isn't anything left for me here either," said Mohamed, the textile shop owner.

"Look at my ancestor's home. There is no life left within the exhausted bricks. "We never imagined Satan would bring hell on us," Mohamed exclaimed, raising his hands in despair to the heavens.

A woman in a Syrian refugee camp

Children playing in a Syrian refugee camp

Chapter 4

The Refugee

At dusk, at the junction of the expressway, a United Nations green bus was transporting asylum seekers towards the Turkish border. Fatima trailed behind Mohamed as he walked towards the bus. She managed to gather whatever belongings she could from the apartment, risking her life in the process.

Donning the gas mask, she attempted to enter the apartment and tried to open the cupboard located in the corner.

She seized a gold necklace from her wedding evening and a sum of money stored in the safe. Without counting the cash, she hastily placed it into her purse, concealed underneath her hijab. Gazing through teary eyes, she surveyed the walls of the apartment, observing their wedding photograph suspended from the wall by a diminutive screw. She hastily placed some garments into her luggage and hurried downstairs towards the street. Access to the apartments was forbidden due to the presence of toxic sarin residue. She passed the restrictive tape at the entrance of the building and spotted Mohamed on the opposite end of the road.

Mohamed paid the bus driver roughly 89,000 Syrian pounds in order to arrange their transportation to the Turkish border. The bus had been stuffed with a large number of ladies and children, leaving very little room. Everyone intended to either go to the Red Cross refugee camp or cross the Turkish border to get food and safeguard the well-being of elderly people and children.

"Look for an appropriate spot to sit. It's already cramped," stated the bus driver from the driver's cabin.

Fatima and Mohamed found a spot in the far back corner of the bus. After about thirty minutes, the bus reached the safe road. As they began their voyage into an uncertain and unforeseen fate, Fatima watched the yellow-reddish skyline of Damascus and the diminishing heights of its apartment buildings against the backdrop of the setting sun, from the window of the backseat. She recalled the delightful view from the balcony of the city she was leaving behind, never to be seen again. As she peeked out of the glass window, she bid farewell to her late husband while witnessing her last view of Damascus and Ghouta.

The bus soon reached the M5 highway and headed toward Aleppo, a city that is situated in northern Syria near the Turkish border. The journey from Goutha to Aleppo was approximately 550 kilometers, and the driver had been determined to make it there without becoming mired in the crossfire between the opposing sides.

The conflict was spreading to Syria's most prominent commercial hub too, which would imminently be plagued by ravaged landmarks—a city bereft of power and residents.
The bus steadily advanced towards the border throughout the whole night, without halting for food or rest.

The driver abruptly changed direction and pulled onto a narrow route shortly before approaching Aleppo.

Fatima heard the sounds of rockets, bombs, and missiles being launched, from a distance. The scene brought back memories of the fireworks on her wedding day.
By dawn, the bus had reached the Red Cross camp situated close to the Turkish border.

Mohamed pointed to the camp and announced, "There it is." We are now inside a secure zone. The camp was set up on an even stretch of desert, filled with several tents, and enclosed by boundaries fortified with wire fencing. The roadways were muddy and dampened as a result of water supplying trucks. The setting depicted an ancient oasis, featuring tents, set against the backdrop of a stunning sunrise in the barren landscape, but filled with stories of sorrow, anger, and death.
Fatima and Mohamed alighted from the bus and approached the camp's entrance. The Red Cross guards stationed at the entrance were positioned with a register and pen to meticulously document the specifics of the refugees. They unlocked the gates and commenced gathering information from the individuals waiting in line. After documenting their details, they were led to a nearby tent.

A middle-aged American woman greeted Fatima.

"Come here, sit on this chair. Please take this package of biscuits and a bottle of water. You appear extremely exhausted," she remarked.

Fatima has no recollection of her most recent meal. Perhaps a man had provided her with a bottle of water while she was at the graveyard. She recalled.
"My spouse perished in a chemical assault," Fatima responded, holding the biscuit pack in her hand and nibbling a piece of it.

The American woman gently touched her head and remarked, "Every individual present here possesses a sorrowful narrative." This camp is replete with calamities and poignant recollections of deprivation and suffering.

Subsequently, she exited the tent in order to mediate a conflict among st the ladies who were contending over rations of food and water.

After resolving the conflict, the American woman came back and discreetly conveyed to Fatima, "Discover a means to acclimate to the camp." There is a sleeping area available in the nearby tent. A girl in that tent had perished due to septic wounds in her abdomen. Assimilate and adhere to the established norms. You see, getting a spot within an excessively populated camp is challenging."

Fatima acclimated to sleeping in the cramped tent over the next days. In the afternoon, they were given a small quantity of biscuits and bread, although the available ration was restricted. She spent her days watching children play outside her tent. But nights were miserable for her. The memories gushed through her mind, making her restless.

One day, a group of children presented her with portions of meat that had been prepared from animals that were dying as a result of famine, in nearby village. They informed her that the animals had perished due to neglect and starvation. Anything would be better than dying of hunger.

One month later, Mohamed, who had been relocated to the male section of the camp, approached her tent accompanied by a gentleman named Abu Hamza. He portrayed Abu Hamza as an individual with remarkable bravery and a loyal companion.

"His means can transport you across the line of control. You will have a happy and better life beyond that border." Mohamed stated.

"Certainly, I am able to assist you in traveling to Istanbul. It is located in Europe. An improved and pleasing life awaits you," Abu Hamza declared, his eyes shimmering with delight at seeing Fatima's resplendent golden necklace.

Fatima understood what Abu Hamza wanted from her.
Fatima removed the golden necklace, which was given to her by her father and had been passed down through multiple generations as an ancestral necklace, and presented it to Abu Hamza.

"There is no need to worry at this moment." Your new passport will be available for collection in seven days. Istanbul is an aesthetically pleasing metropolis renowned for its iconic monuments and lavish life. "You will be safe in that location," Abu reassured her, feeling the gold necklace in his hand.

"It will fetch a substantial sum." He murmured.

However, Fatima lost herself in her thoughts.

She recalled teaching her students about Istanbul, including its violent past, historical conflicts, the renowned Hagia Sophia, and the iconic Blue Mosque. From now on, this country will serve as her permanent residence.

A week later, Abu Hamza arrived at the camp, carrying Fatima's recently acquired fake Turkish passport. Upon opening it, she discovered her new appellation: Noor Mohamed Shanbeg, with her photo pasted on the page.

Abu summoned her to the camp gates at midnight in order to cross to the opposite side of the border. They entered Turkey at the border town of Akçakale in the Şanlıurfa province.

But, Mohamed returned to the Red Cross camp after escorting her to the border. He desired to pass away in his native land, fighting against the government forces.

Abu led Fatima to a nearby merchant who specializes in spices. The shop's name was 'Turk Spice Company.'

"This is Mr. Ozel," Abu stated, indicating at Ozel with a handshake gesture.

"He will serve as your mentor in this country," he said.

Ozel grinned at her, revealing his fractured incisor.

"Hello, my dear," he greeted.
"I have made the necessary arrangements for you to travel to Istanbul." You have the opportunity to be employed as a translator at a tourism company. Here are your bus tickets. You have to depart for the city tomorrow. There are numerous Syrian girls employed at the location. There are women present in the room on the first floor. Some of them will depart tomorrow. Meanwhile, you have the option to stay overnight on the upper floor with them," he said.

"Ok". Fatima replied, reaching for the wooden stairs to the first floor.

The room, a big hall was filled with many girls wearing hijab. Fatima's vision was limited to the hazel eyes of the individuals, which were brimming with a sense of hopelessness.

"It is the sole desire of Allah for us," expressed a woman of middle age seated in the corner.

"Please, have a seat here, in the corner," she said to Fatima. "You appear exceedingly fatigued."

Throughout the night, she listened the narratives of young women hailing from various regions of Syria, including Aleppo, Homs, Damascus, Ghouta, Raqqa, and Latakia. Two women had a young daughter alongside them. They had completed their education up to primary school. A group of adolescent girls ranging in age from 14 to 18 years were also in the room.

Many of the young women aspired to amass great wealth in urban areas of Turkey, with no intention of ever returning to their country. No one desired to revisit the agonizing recollections of the past. Some girls simply wanted to stay in the nearby city until the end of the war and then return to their native city. Few girls simply desired to go back, endure the suffering, and fight alongside rebels.

Fatima reflected, "Fortunately, my father provided me with an education. What will be the fate of these young, naive females who have yet to see the bustling metropolis? They lack the ability to read anything other than lines from the holy book. What does the future, which seemed grim and unpredictable to me, have in store for them?"

Throughout the night, the sound of someone sobbing could be heard emanating from behind the opaque black curtain on the face.

On the following day, Fatima embarked on the bus bound for Istanbul. The remaining girls were likewise sent to different cities across the country.

Istanbul

Chapter 5

Istanbul

Fatima arrived in Istanbul, a historic cosmopolitan metropolis, the following day. The ancient city walls had witnessed the deaths of warriors and innumerable wars. Death had become an integral component of her existence. The soil had been saturated with the blood of numerous deceased soldiers, and the rain had subsequently deposited it into the salted waters of the Bosphorus. Ultimately, blood is also salted. No distinction exists between them; humans have also observed no distinction.

As Fatima alighted from the bus at Sultanahmet, she was able to observe the majestic dome of Hagia Sophia and the minarets of the stunning Blue Mosque from the road.

"That is it." Only photographs and my historical texts have permitted me to see it. The tales I instructed children in class encompassed all of this. Who would have imagined that I would be present to witness the realization of my stories? I wish Ahmed were present," she stated to herself.

Suddenly, a tingling sensation was accompanied by a sharp, lancinating pain that shot through her cranium. She perched on her suitcase after putting it down.

She briefly experienced an impairment of vision; however, the discomfort dissipated almost immediately.

"It is possible that I did not get enough sleep last night." She pondered the possibility that this might have been the reason behind it. She pulled out the tourist company's business card and summoned a yellow taxi.

"Merhaba brother, Nasılsın?" she asked the driver in Turkish. "Can you take me to the Taksim Square?"

The driver left her off at the square, and she proceeded to the small street near the bus stand. She strolled down the street carrying her suitcase, tracking the map on the paper note.

As she paused in front of 'Hotel Pera', Fatima noticed a well-decorated 'Bosphorus Tourist Guides' office across the street.

She approached the office through the glass door and noticed a man in his fifties, fiddling with his cell phone. He had an unkempt face and noticeable forehead wrinkles.

She approached the reception desk and spoke to that person, stating, "Hello, I am Fatima.....I mean Noor from Syria."
The man looked confused as he glanced up. "What?" he asked.
She reiterated, "I stated that I came from Syria."
The guy gazed at her while scratching his beard.

"Evet, he apprised me that you would be coming from Syria. Are you alone, or are there other girls with you?" he asked.
"What is your name, manager?"Do you know Ozel? Fatima inquired, slightly surprised.

"Mehmet, okay now I remember now," he replied.

"It is a pleasure to meet you," he said. "Sit down and relax." I will notify him of your arrival by cellphone. In the meantime, please go over the contract paperwork and fill out this form.
He talked with a person on his cellphone and presented her with documents.

She started reading the contract while reclining on the desk.

Mehmet informed the person on the phone, "Yes, Mr. Ozel, she has reached."

Fatima signed the contract without considering most of its contents.

"The previous guide we had came from Libya. She resided in Dolapdere Square. You are welcome to stay there. Each month, the rent is 1600 TL," he said.

Mehmet handed her an old piece of paper containing the flat address.

"Here are the keys. It's not that far from her," he told her.

"All right, I will see you at 9:00 a.m. tomorrow. A new group of American tourists would be arriving tomorrow," he further stated.

Fatima eagerly proceeded to get some rest in her new apartment. The apartment was small, with a single room along with an attached kitchen.

She reported to the company office the following day to begin her job as an assistant guide. For a few months, she worked as an assistant to an old lady guide, who was a migrant from Cyprus. She quickly learned the historical details of the city's monuments.

After a couple of months, she started working as an independent guide.

Hagia Sophia

Chapter 6

Noor-e-Shams

After two months, Fatima was struggling to make ends meet on her minuscule salary. She had to pay 1600 TL to live in the apartment offered by the company. The remaining amount of her wage went toward living expenses. On Sundays, she headed to the bazaar to buy secondhand garments for the upcoming winter.
With no companions, she took some stray cats from the street and raised them as her family. Days passed while she worked and brought food to her new pals.

It had been six months since she had last spoken to her folks. She last spoke to them at the refugee camp. Her parents were also moved to a nearby mosque for safety. And her brother married the cobbler's daughter after promising her father not to fight in war.

She reached out to her parents via the company-provided cellphone. Her parents rejoiced when she informed them that she had received a job in Istanbul.

Her father told that her mother's diabetes was getting worse, and she was barely able to walk. Her father took her to the city's sole functioning hospital, as many had been destroyed by the continuing battle. Her brother, who now had a little family to care for, had taken up an odd occupation as a cab driver. The doctor advised them that her mother's leg was swollen and the infection was bad. They suggested an early amputation of the limb, to save her life. Her brother begged for assistance for the procedure. Fatima's salary was 3500 TL, but after paying 1600 TL in rent and 1400 TL in food and clothing, she could only save 500 TL for each month.
Desperate to support her family, she raced to the "döviz" [money exchange] at Dolapadre Square to transfer 4000 TL, her savings, to her father. On her way home, she picked up some leftovers from a nearby restaurant for her kitties.
Sitting on her bed, she thought about earning more to support her family. Portraits of the beautiful Girl Guide in office albums rushed through her head.

She knew what she needed to do to support her family.

"I need to do this extra work to help my family," she said quietly to herself.

But self-doubt set in. "I'm so shy and have never done this before."

The next evening, she prepared for her new work. She donned a revealing red second-hand gown she found at the Sunday bazaar and applied lipstick and blush.

She closed the door to her room, left some food for her animals, and went to Taksim Square.

Taksim Square was overcrowded with tourists. One of them, a portly man in shorts, approached her and asked, "Would you like to have a relationship with me?"

Fatima nodded, hoping to collect 2000 TL in return, which she intended to transfer to her mother through the 'hawala' route.

"Where are you from?" she questioned.

"United States, Los Angeles," the man answered.

"Ah, LA," Fatima murmured.

They walked to a nearby hotel together. Fatima wanted to forget the next few hours of her life. After an hour, the man got up and buttoned his shorts. "What's your name?" he inquired.

"Fati... umm... Noor," she stuttered. "Yes, my name is Noor—Noor-e-Shams."

"Yes, Noor-e-Shams," she replied carefully.

She swiftly accepted the money offered and seized a taxi back to her apartment. Once inside, she shut herself in the bathroom, letting the shower cleanse away her regrets. She sat under the water, shedding tears.

After an hour, she put on her clothes, retrieved her purse, and counted the cash she had received. She felt worn out and slept in her bed till the next day. The next day, she dashed to the döviz and transferred the money to her mother through the hawala channel.

Back at the tourist office, her mind was still replaying her new name, Noor-e-Shams……………… Noor-e-Shams………. Noor-e-Shams.

Noor-e-Shams carried on with her new life for the next few months, finding new clients around Taksim Square.

She continued to send money to her mother and brother in order to help pay for her mother's diabetic medications and support her brother's family.

Her brother continued to work as a taxi driver, braving the perils of a war-torn country where even friends were turning into enemies.

Konya

Mevlana museum

Chapter 7

John

John was a thirty-something year-old man. His family had come from Lebanon, bringing with them their Syrian Orthodox faith. He was reared in Dora, Lebanon, but his father migrated to Konya, Anatolia, many years ago in the pursuit of better opportunities. Lebanon was plagued by a bloody civil war then, which forced his father to find a new town to raise the family.
Konya, an old and culturally rich city, was John's new home.
John and his elderly mother resided in a humble house beside the Mevlana Mosque. His father died in a car accident when John was attending graduate school. Before his death, John's father worked as a cleaner at the mosque and hoped that John would join the military to serve his new country.
After graduation, John attended the military naval academy, leaving his mother in the care of his aunt. John was a calm and serene individual with a thorough comprehension of the universe's laws. Despite their terrible poverty, he always smiled warmly, like a lotus blossoming in a swamp, unaffected by the filth below.

His father used to say, "John is my gem worth a billion dollars."

John's tranquil manner was frequently compared to that of a Rumi disciple, representing the calmness and wisdom of Konya.
John joined the Turkish Navy after graduating from the Karamürselbey Training Center and was assigned to the Black Sea Fleet. His employment took him to Zonguldak, a quiet naval station town on the Black Sea.

After a year of service and training, he took a five-day break and came to Istanbul to finish paperwork at the naval command in Anadolukavağı. Following that, he checked into the lovely, turquoise-painted 4th April Hotel in Sultanahmet, which overlooks the Bosphorus Straits.
The young Azerbaijani attendant graciously led him to his room in the hotel. After a long bus ride, John easily fell asleep. That evening, he sipped tea at the hotel's rooftop café while admiring the stunning sea views.
"Merhaba, are you visiting Istanbul for the first time?" the receptionist asked.
"Yes," John responded.
"You should go to Taksim Square, which is a short walk from here. It's a bustling area with plenty of tourists and retailers. I stayed there when I initially came to Turkey," the young man stated with fondness.
"Humm, tamam," John responded.
He changed into casual clothes and left the hotel, wandering along the shore. The

fresh, chilly breeze stroked against his face, and he felt profoundly content. "I had always wanted to visit this city.

He reminisced, "I had always wanted to visit this city. Mother always wanted to see the majestic Hagia Sophia, the seat of our faith and the ruler of the ancient Christian world."

He used a map from the hotel reception to navigate to Hagia Sophia and then acquired a taxi to Taksim Square. He sat on a bench among the crowded streets lined with shops and restaurants, tying his loose shoelaces.

When he looked up, a tall, fair woman with beautiful, curly hair approached him. She walked gracefully and whispered, "Merhaba." Sorry, ahh... Hello. How are you? Are you a tourist here?

John nodded.

"I am Noor-e-Shams. I work as a tour guide and a translator. I can speak English, Turkish, and Arabic. Would you like to have my services?" she inquired, passing him her card.

"A nice card..." Noor-e-Shams has beautiful eyes. "What does it mean?" John inquired.

"Noor signifies 'light' in Arabic. So it means 'Light of Shams' or 'Light of Syria,'" she said.

"Yes, I need a friend to show me around the city," John told me.

"That will be 200 dollars," Noor-e-Shams stated, demonstrating her trust.

"Okay, let's go," John said.

They went through the medieval city's small streets, with Noor-e-Shams discussing the city's historical significance in her terrible English with Arabic accent. They saw the magnificent Hagia Sophia and the stunning Blue Mosque. Throughout the tour, John's attention was centered on her.

As nightfall fell, the ferries and boats along the shore were illuminated with beautiful decorations. They purchased a dining cruise ticket, which was smaller and less well-lit than the other alternatives. They sipped Turkish wine at a candlelit table while watching Turkish dancers perform to fascinating music. As a vintage tune played, the environment became calmer.

They climbed onto the boat's deck and embraced each other as the cool air brushed over their cheeks. They watched the cruise glide past the illuminated Istanbul Bridge, accompanied by a flock of seagulls chirping in the silence of the sea.

John took a big breath as the full moon appeared behind the Blue Mosque's towering minarets and exclaimed, "If heaven exists, it is here in love. A garden stands in between right and wrong. I'll meet you there."

"Both happiness and misery exist in the present moment. What are they fighting for?" Noor-e-Shams responded.
They clasped hands and listened to the waves as the boat docked. They took a taxi to Dolapdere Square, where Noor-e-Shams resided in a small, ancient building. The flat was modest, consisting of a bedroom and a kitchen. A white Turkish cat rested on the balcony.
"This is John, Habibi," Noor-e-Shams introduced him to the feline.

"And, John, here's 'Prini,' my younger sister. She's my only family here," she said.

After freshening up, John sat on the kitchen couch while Noor-e-Shams made tea. As she discussed her life back in Syria.

She stated, "I work as a part-time prostitute here to support my family in Syria. They pay me $200 per hour, which I save and give to my old parents via the 'döviz.' My parents believe I have a good job in this prosperous city."
She broke down as she told her story.

"Everyone is an enemy of each other back in Syria," she said as her voice ached with the images of the past.
"Don't worry; everything will be fine," John said to her, grasping her hands. He kissed her forehead and drew her closer. Their hearts raced as their warm breaths mixed together. John tenderly kissed her lips and pulled her into the bedroom.
The next morning, the first rays of sunlight filtered through the window slats. After weeks of rain in Istanbul, Noor-e-Shams woke to the sight of sunshine.

It had been a wonderful night, and she felt a profound feeling of peace and fulfillment.
She rose softly, turned on the kettle, and opened the kitchen window. As she watched John sleep peacefully, she looked at him and again got immersed in her past.

"Don't look back." Nobody knows how the world began. Don't be afraid of the future; nothing lasts forever. "If you think about the past or the future, you will miss the moment," John said, echoing in her ears.
"I didn't know you were an early riser. She said.
"Because of your love, I have broken with my past," John said softly as she poured him a cup of tea.
"Get up, John. I'm your tour guide, remember? We have many more locations to explore.

I'll make breakfast. I have eggs for omelets," Noor-e-Shams said.
"Okay, as you wish," John replied.

They visited additional historic places across the city, and John reserved tickets for a Turkish Dervish play at Hudapasha in the evening. The Sufi dervish dance at the Mevlana Museum in Konya had long captivated him.

"John, why do you want to watch the Dervishes dance?"Can't you enjoy yourself at a pub or a dance club?" Noor-e-Shams inquired.

"Dance when you're broken open." If you have torn the bandage off, dance. Dance in the middle of a fight. Dance in your blood. I feel that dervish dance and music shatter our egos. We succumb to the universe's dance. This struggle and battle are the result of our egos. Those who do not comprehend the universe's intelligence and love fight irrationally," John explained.

After the show, they walked to Taksim Square's for dinner at 'Rehyun', an Iranian restaurant. Noor-e-Shams observed beggars and homeless children on the small dark lane leading to the restaurant.
"Look, John. They're from Syria. "They had plenty to eat before the war broke out," she explained.
John took out 200 lira and handed it to a woman holding a newborn.
"Why help her?" Noor-e-Shams inquired.
"I am not sure how it will assist, but even a small act of compassion could make a difference. John responded, "You never know what destiny has in store for her."
At the restaurant, John placed his order for Persian food and opened a small wooden box. He looked at Noor-e-Shams and said, "I really like you." I want to make you my lifelong partner. When I return from my current posting, I hope to marry you. This jewelry belonged to my mother. I want you to keep it as a symbol of our connection."

Noor-e-Shams was stunned and perplexed. "This is called 'zina' in our religion. You are Christian, while I am Muslim. How can we marry?"
"I do not belong to any faith. My faith is love. John said, "Every heart is my religion."
"But people out there are dangerous and don't respect love and humanity," Noor-e-Shams added.
"Some things are beyond human comprehension. The universe follows its own laws. "Human intervention cannot change that," John stated.
"Habibi, I love you, but sometimes I don't understand what you say," she said,

taking the necklace and draping it around her neck. "It looks beautiful, doesn't it?"

Then, they held hands and just became silent, watching the ferries cross the strait until John's bus to Çanakkale arrived.

Mediterranean Sea

Chapter 8

Admiral. Rustom Pasha

The next day, John reported to the base and joined the submarine fleet. The kilo-class submarine was scheduled to be stationed on the eastern Mediterranean seafront. The beautiful "TCG Pirireis" stood above the water, her name etched on her neck. John looked at the lovely whale-like machine, kissed it, and hopped onto the deck. He was welcomed by a tall officer with bushy mustache and wide shoulders. John noticed his tall stature and the name 'Admiral. Rustom Pasha' on his nameplate.
"Welcome, John, aboard. This will be your home for the next six months, and we are your family, young lad."
I am pleased that your community is fighting for our beautiful homeland.
Within the chambers, the submarine resembled a hobbit's dwelling. John immediately acclimated to his new surroundings and responsibilities.

They began sailing towards the shore of Latakia in Syria. John became acquainted with the numerous ammunitions provided in the submarine. He rapidly compiled a list of everything available in the capsule. They cruised towards the border both to conduct reconnaissance and as a deterrent.

The Mediterranean waters appeared elegantly, blue, and heavenly. However, it was windy and turbulent.

For John, the night was especially conducive to self reflection. In the silence of the night, he used to think about his encounter with Noor and living a future life with her. He used to reflect on the world he was born in. He used to wonder about the universe, the stars, and its immensity. He would sometimes become engrossed in thinking of everyday things in life. At times, his intellect was clouded by the idea of his life's mission.
However, Admiral Pasha appeared to be a sensible and composed man to him. He could sense the sensitivity of the guy underlying his roughness. He possessed the discipline of a conscious individual.

After months of reconnaissance, they received orders to mount an attack on the enemy. John soon devised plans to deploy torpedoes and missiles from the vessel.
It was John's first assault on an adversary, yet it raised additional doubts in his mind, and he badly sought answers.
After weeks of being in international seas and after the operation were

completed, John finally had the opportunity to speak with the admiral.
One day, the admiral summoned him for a brief conference in the navigation chambers.

"You know, John, I'm also from the Konya district. My village is not distant from Konya. I was delighted that you are from the same township. Konya left me with some lovely memories. You are a Christian working for the country. That is the beauty of Ataturk's country. He understood how the universe's laws worked. He understood that humans associate with the geographic place in which they grow and nurture their upbringing. A country can be formed not through religion, but through the feelings of its people. Even within a family, people have various beliefs and ways of thinking. They have both conflicts and pleasant moments. It is a universal law. Nothing is the same. Different people, minds, animals, plants, stars, and planet systems. It is the universe's way of acquiring information and growing, just as humans do from birth to old age. There are different frames of moments in a continuum. However, there is a sense of oneness as one being.
Humm..... But John, you occasionally appear puzzled; what's the matter? He asked.

But, sir, what's the purpose of life? John asked.

Pasha grinned and said, "The aim of life is to cultivate the mind and cleanse it of greed and bitterness. The universe understands and knows itself. The goal is to become one with the universe and possess a universal mind.

But, sir, we are army men; we kill our opponents and receive medals for valor. John responded.

Humm..., we battle to rescue our country and its people. We don't fight with anger in our hearts. When we fight our opponents, we do so to protect our motherland but we also have of compassion and love for their families. That is our courage. We do it because destiny has given it upon us.

"Yes, sir, I guess I received my replies. Many thanks". John replied and exited the room.
Back in his room, he began packing his suitcases, excited to meet Noor.

Whirling Dervishes

Chapter 9

Rumi

It had been a year since John had seen Noor and he was pleased to finally take a two-month sabbatical. He had purchased a bus ticket from Golcuk to Istanbul and was looking forward to seeing Noor and discussing their future plans. He woke up as; he smelled the strong odor of the city's smoke.

He arrived early in the morning in month January in a windy, rainy day. The rain-soaked streets and biting winds were in sharp contrast to the warm, welcoming city when he came last time. He recalled. And immediately took a taxi to Dolapdere Square.
"It is early. I should be able to catch her at home before she goes to work," he assured the Nigerian cab driver.
The driver looked back, puzzled by John's optimism.
When John arrived at Noor's flat, he discovered just her cat, Prini, on the doorstep. The door was locked.
He knocked on the adjoining flat's door, and an elderly lady opened it.
"Merhaba, can you tell me where the girl who lived next to you is?" he asked her.
"Oh, I haven't seen her for months. But when her business manager arrived to lock the flat, he indicated that she was in a refugee hospital," the elderly lady explained.

"But this cat comes daily to her doorsteps and I am fed up with feeding her."She said angrily.

John picked up the cat and rushed to the square nearby.
John asked a taxi driver at the square for the address of the Syrian refugee hospital and directed the cab driver to take him there with the cat on his lap.

At the hospital, John raced to the reception desk, where a Syrian woman was sitting.
"Merhaba, I am seeking a girl named Noor. She came here for some treatment," he told the receptionist.
The receptionist scanned her computer screen and discovered no record of Noor.
"Please check again. "She's a young woman, 27 years old, with dark black curly hair," John said.
The receptionist nodded. "Yes, there are some young women admitted to the gynecology section."It is on the third floor."
John hurried to the elevator and headed to the gynecology department. He saw

Noor lying on a corner bed in the general ward.
He swiftly approached Noor's bed after asking the chief nurse for permission to see her. Rumi, the girl child with gorgeous blue eyes similar to John's, lay next to her.
As the baby stirred, Noor opened her eyes and recognized John.
"Salam, mister, Who are you? You look familiar. Do I know you? Are you a friend?" She asked.

John was taken aback. "My name is John, Noor. Don't you remember me? What has happened to you? "Why are you in the hospital?"

The head nurse interrupted. "Mister, Dr. Hashim wants to see you. His office is located on the ground floor.

John visited Dr. Hashim's office. Hello, Doctor. "I'm John."
Dr. Hashim offered his hand. "We have been waiting for you, John. It's been a while since someone paid her a visit. Noor has been here for three months, after giving birth to her baby girl. We have been caring for both her and the baby."
He reached beneath his desk and brought out a portrait. "Noor brought this portrait with her to the hospital. I feel it is of you. The eyes are strikingly similar."
John stared at the portrait, Noor had drawn.

At the footnote she had written "With love from Syria".

"John, Noor is sick. She has Creutzfeldt-Jakob disease (CJD) and dementia, which have led to memory loss. Her illness is degenerative and affects her muscles. We're not sure how much longer she has to endure life."
John's eyes filled up with tears.

"Doctor, I'd like to take my daughter and her mother home," after a while, he inquired.

Dr Hashim nodded in affirmation.

Returning to the ward, John cradled Rumi in his lap while she smiled at him.

"Let's go home, our sweet home in Konya," he added gently.

Noor appeared puzzled. "Why do you appear so familiar? What is your name, region, and religion? Anyway, I am bored here. Nobody speaks to me, and this young kid cries a lot. "She is always hungry."
John said with a sweet smile, "Yes, my religion is the same as the newborn girl's."

"Let's go home," Noor said, clutching his finger as if it served as a lifeline for some more time.

Homs,(Syria)[city center] after the war

Chapter 10

Dr. Hashim

Once having a thriving practice in Homs, seasoned gynecologist Dr. Hashim, in his sixties, enjoyed it, but his life was turned upside down when conflict tore at his native country. Along with physical injuries, he lost his wife and only son in a bomb explosion close by their house. Driven by growing strife, he finally sought safety in Istanbul and started working in a refugee hospital.

He had a subdued first meeting with Noor. Reporting a slight fever and headaches, she arrived at his clinic carrying a refugee ID given by the UN. Then he was working as a general physician because of staff shortages in the overwhelmed hospital. Dr. Hashim just wrote prescriptions for antibiotics and painkillers.

Noor came back a month later, now beset with terrible headaches and disturbing memory problems.

"Dr. Hashim, I'm not sure where my apartment or the surrounding areas are. I frequently find myself knocking on the doors of strangers," she complained.

Concerned, Dr. Hashim directed an MRI scan, a battery of blood tests, and hormone level checks. After examining the findings and discussing them with colleagues, he diagnosed Noor with multiple sclerosis (MS).

"No....o, though my colleagues think you have MS, I'm not really sure. To delay the course of the illness, you will have to begin an injection and medicine regimen." He told Noor.

"Doctor, is this medication expensive?" Noor questioned.
"Indeed. It is expensive" Dr. Hashim replied.
"I don't have enough money now. Okay, I'll come back tomorrow for the injections," Noor remarked.

She anxiously departed from the hospital, her mind drifted to John, whom she had met just a month ago.

As she left, she silently said, "Oh, John, I wish you were here."

Returning home, Noor contacted her father. "Baba, for a few months I won't be able to send money. Fewer vacationers this season means less due from my company. Tell Nasser to look for some more jobs and assist you, please." She told him.

Noor started her treatment at the hospital the following day, using her savings to pay for the necessary medication.
Noor's condition deteriorated over time. She stopped having her periods and battled to keep her usual working schedule. She was told it was a side effect of the MS medicine when she brought this up with a nurse.
Noor's confused moments of memory loss were increasingly common, even with therapy.

In her sound heath, she used to paint views of Istanbul from her fleeting stay with John and a portrait of John. She left a portion of the portrait unpainted, unable to remember the precise form of his lips.

Growing increasingly concerned about Noor's worsening condition and frequent depression episodes, Dr. Hashim asked a friend in the United States who was a neurologist for advice. After reviewing Noor's records and background, the neurologist called Dr. Hashim with a diagnosis.
"Hashim, I think this is a rare instance of Creutzfeldt-Jakob Disease (CJD), sometimes known as CJD here, in the United States. She most certainly picked it from tainted meat in the refugee camps," He said.

Understanding the seriousness of the matter, Dr. Hashim now understood how Noor's symptoms related to her illness.

Noor's abdomen started to exhibit a clear bump, suggesting conception, as the condition developed. Noor's hold on reality kept slipping away, irrespective of her increasing bodily changes. Her medical trips clearly revealed her bewilderment and disorientation.

Dr. Hashim noted her increasing difficulty comprehending her circumstances. Frustrated at last, he shouted at her "Where did this come from? This is under whose responsibility? How would you take care of yourself and this baby?"

But, Noor stayed blank, lost in her own universe.
Concerned for both Noor and her unborn child, Dr. Hashim requested more blood tests and an ultrasound. He requested the hospital director to admit Noor to a female ward, explaining her appalling conditions. They gave her an empty corner bed so that she would get appropriate treatment and support for both her child and herself.

Nubian Pyramids on a Desert in Sudan

Chapter 11

Zulu, 7th, July 2031

It's been only a year, but I am feeling that I haven't seen her in ages, and the anticipation in my heart is almost intolerable. She was my best friend for a decade, and now, as the stars shine above and the Mevlana shrine stands majestically before me, I am overwhelmed with recollections of our shared past.

We grew up together under this sky, playing in the shadows and murmurs of the Mevlana Museum courtyard. Last year, we said goodbye here, right before she moved to Istanbul to pursue her ambition of becoming a neurologist. It was a time fraught with both optimism and grief.

My family and I fled the atrocities of the civil war in North Sudan, finding a precarious haven in Konya. In 2023, we traveled through the treacherous waters of the Mediterranean Sea. Many died in the other boats that sailed through the Libyan coast when their boats were capsized in the stormy sea. We were lucky to survive and landed on the Turkish coast.

My father took on a menial job as a sweeper at the museum, a symbol of our fresh beginning amid broken dreams. As for me, I've been engrossed in my engineering studies, adjusting to life apart from the place we left behind.

Rumi and I met ten years ago, on this very day—July 7th. Her world was destroyed the day she lost her mother. Every year since, she has come here with her father; bearing pink roses as a heartfelt tribute to the woman she lost too soon.

Today, the weight of that shared past is almost tangible. I'm here, waiting with bated breath, to finally see her again. She appears from a distance, a beacon against the backdrop of the mosque. She clutches her father's hand and carries a bouquet of vivid roses that appear to pulse with the spirit of her feelings. Her eyes, sparkling with whispered stories and silent strength, meet mine. Her smile is a blend of serenity and wisdom, as if time has collapsed into this single moment of reunion.

As she gets closer, the years between us appear to fade, leaving only the strong bond we once shared. The air is charged with the excitement of this long-awaited experience, and in this hallowed space, our history and present collide in a breathtaking panorama of optimism and nostalgia.

The end

You rave about the Holy Place (Masjid al-Haram) and say you've visited God's garden, but where is your bunch of flowers? There is some merit in the suffering you have endured, but what a pity you have not discovered the Makkah that is inside.

"Every war and every conflict between human beings has happened because of some disagreement about names. It is such an unnecessary foolishness, because just beyond the arguing there is a long table of companionship set and waiting for us to sit down. What is praised is one, so the praise is one too, many jugs being poured into a huge basin. All religions, all this singing one song. The differences are just illusion and vanity. Sunlight looks a little different on this wall than it does on that wall and a lot different on this other one, but it is still one light. We have borrowed these clothes, these time-and-space personalities, from a light, and when we praise, we are pouring them back in."

— Jalal ad-Din Rumi

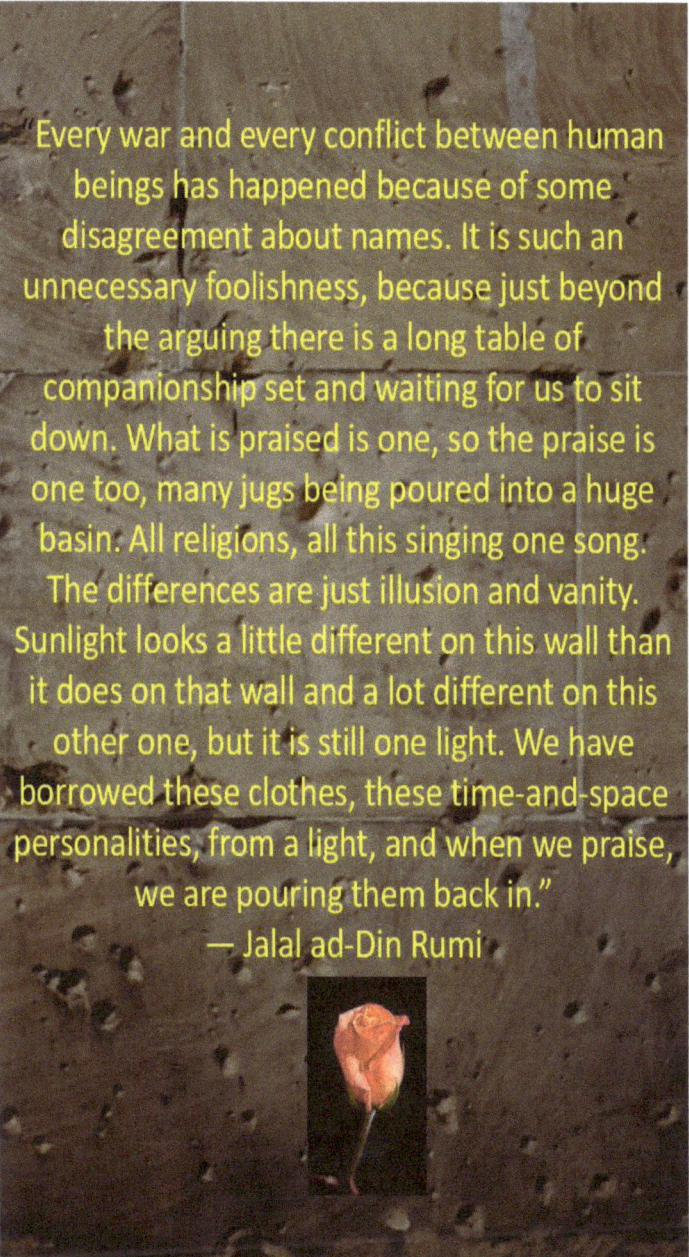

About the Author-

"Snehaal Kemal" is the literary name of this author. The author is a maxillofacial surgeon currently living in India. He has been writing medical articles and has ventured into writing fictional stories with this piece of work.

www.ingramcontent.com/pod-product-compliance
Lightning Source LLC
LaVergne TN
LVHW061626070526
838199LV00070B/6596